Visit us on the Web!
www.randomhouse.com/kids

Educators and librarians, for a variety of teaching tools, visit us at
www.randomhouse.com/teachers

*Library of Congress Cataloging-in-Publication Data*
Eastman, Peter.
Fred and Ted's road trip / by Peter Eastman. — 1st ed.
  p. cm.
Summary: Dogs Fred and Ted pack up their cars and go on a road trip, and their different ways of doing things have interesting results.
ISBN 978-0-375-86764-4 (trade) — ISBN 978-0-375-96764-1 (lib. bdg.) — ISBN 978-0-375-89854-9 (ebook)
[1. Automobile travel—Fiction. 2. Friendship—Fiction. 3. Individuality—Fiction. 4. Dogs—Fiction.] I. Title.
PZ7.E13153Frs 2011 [E]—dc22 2010006265

Printed in the United States of America
10 9 8
First Edition

# Fred and Ted's Road Trip

## by Peter Eastman

BEGINNER BOOKS®

A Division of Random House, Inc.

Fred and Ted were going on a road trip.

Ted packed the lunch.

Fred packed the tools.

They drove away.

Ted drove on the road.

Fred drove on the grass.

They came to a big mud puddle.
Fred drove into it.

Ted drove around it.

They stopped at a water hose.

Ted was clean.

Fred was dirty.

Ted turned on the water.

He stayed dry.

Fred got wet.

They came to a log.

Fred drove over it.

Ted drove under it.

They stopped to have a picnic.

Ted carried the lunch.

Fred spread the blanket.

They sat down to eat.

Ted felt one drop.

Fred felt two drops.

It started to rain!
Ted ran to his red car.

Fred ran to his green car.

Ted drove in the rain.

Fred drove out of the rain.

They drove in the desert.

Ted was cool.

Fred was hot.

They ran over some cactus.

Fred got a flat tire.

In the toolbox,

Ted found a pump.

Fred found a spoon.

Ted pumped.

Fred found apples.

Ted pumped and pumped and pumped!

Fred found bread and milk and a pineapple!

Fred went up and up and up!

Fred called for help from up in the air.

Ted raced to help down on the ground.

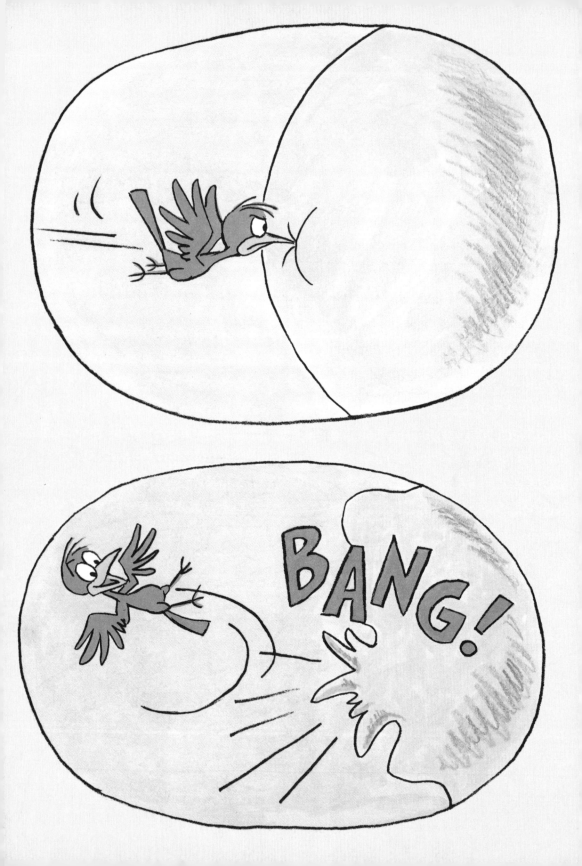

The bird stayed up.

Fred went down.

Back at home, safe and sound!
Did they finish their picnic?

Yes! They did.

Ted had a sandwich.

Fred had a hard-boiled egg and a pickle.

Peter Eastman is the son of P. D. Eastman (1909–1986), author/illustrator of *Are You My Mother?*, *Go, Dog. Go!*, *The Best Nest*, and many other beloved children's books.

Peter followed his father into the animation field, working as an award-winning animator/director. This is his third book featuring the characters Fred and Ted.